#6 PEANUT IN CHARGE

Look for these and other books
in the PEANUT BUTTER
AND JELLY series:

#6 PEANUT IN CHARGE

Dorothy Haas

Illustrated by Jeffrey Lindberg

A
LITTLE APPLE
PAPERBACK

SCHOLASTIC INC.
New York Toronto London Auckland Sydney

ISBN 0-590-42391-6

12 11 10 9 8 7 6 5 4 3 2 1   9/8 0 1 2 3/9

Printed in the U.S.A.   11

First Scholastic printing, December 1989

CHAPTER
1

Peanut finished cutting up an apple onto her cereal. Reaching for a banana, she pulled back the skin and sliced the fruit on top of the apple.

Her sister Maggie put down her spoon, watching.

Going to the refrigerator, Peanut found a plastic bowl of fruit cocktail. "Can I have some of this?" she asked over her shoulder.

Mrs. Butterman nodded absentmindedly. She was reading the morning paper. "Just be sure to leave enough to put on our cottage cheese salad for lunch tomorrow," she murmured.

Peanut returned to the table and spooned some of the fruit into her cereal-apple-banana bowl. She topped it off with a single cherry and poured milk into the bowl around the edges, careful not to undo her handiwork. There! She took a big spoonful. Yummm! What a wonderful way to start a Saturday.

"*Mo-om!*" Maggie managed to make two sounds of that simple word. "Just look at that!"

Mrs. Butterman glanced up from the paper. "What, dear?"

Maggie pointed at Peanut's heaping bowl. "She's going to eat that huge bowlful of stuff. And she's got peanut butter on her toast. And she's getting fat. And — "

"Margaret!" Mrs. Butterman said sharply.

"I'm not fat," protested Peanut. "Poppy says I'm just pleasingly plump." Poppy was Grandfather Wayne.

"What Polly is eating is all perfectly fine — wonderful, in fact — for a girl of her age. She's growing and needs energy," said Mrs. Butterman.

"*I'll* say she's growing," grumbled Maggie, who had been complaining a lot about Peanut lately. "You should've seen her yesterday at Thirty-one Flavors. She had this triple-dipper ice-cream cone. Three scoops!"

"It's *my* allowance," Peanut said good-naturedly. "If I want to save up and have three scoops one day instead of one scoop on three days, what difference does it make?"

"Because it's gross," said Maggie.

"It is not!" said Peanut. "It's good."

"Girls!" Mrs. Butterman sighed. "Let's not start a nice Saturday with bickering. Maggie, I'd rather you didn't point out Polly's eating habits at mealtime. It only spoils her enjoyment and accomplishes nothing."

"It doesn't spoil my breakfast one bit," said Peanut. "This tastes scrumptious." She added after a minute, "I wonder what it would taste like with maple syrup on it instead of milk."

"Clear that with me before you try it," said Mrs. Butterman.

Somehow, Peanut got the idea her mother wouldn't approve of maple syrup on three-kinds-of-fruit and cereal.

Nibbsie, Peanut's little curly-haired dog, barked. Yip. He scratched at the kitchen door.

4

"Pretty soon, Nibbs," Peanut promised. "It's beginning to snow," she told her mother. "I hope we get piles and piles."

"Not before tonight," said Mrs. Butterman. "Not until I get home from the Loop." She meant downtown Chicago. Everybody called it the "Loop."

"It'll be so pretty," said Peanut. "And fun. I haven't made a snowman since last winter in Minneapolis." Minneapolis seemed like a long, long time ago.

"There isn't as much snow here as there used to be back home," said Maggie. "I wish there was."

"Home," Mrs. Butterman said thoughtfully. She patted Maggie's hand. "This is home now." She studied Maggie's face. "You're still missing Minneapolis."

"It's nice here," Maggie admitted. "I like the kids. Our swimming team is great. But I miss Minneapolis sometimes. I miss skiing."

"We'll go back to see Aunt Jean next summer," promised Mrs. Butterman.

"But there won't be any snow then," said Maggie.

Nibbsie yipped again. Yip. And again. Yip yip.

"All right already! I'm coming," said Peanut, scraping her bowl and stuffing one last bite of toast into her mouth. She carried her dishes to the sink and was starting to rinse them when the telephone rang. She dropped the dishes with a clatter and raced Maggie to the phone in the front hall. She won.

"Butterman residence," she said politely. "Polly speaking."

It was Mrs. McCune from down the block. "Is your mother there?" she asked. Something in her voice sounded as though she were upset.

Maggie went back to her breakfast and Mrs. Butterman came to the telephone. Peanut went to the closet to look for her boots, as Nibbsie scampered around her feet.

Mrs. Butterman listened for a minute. "Ohhhhh," she said, sounding sorry. "That *is* a problem. I don't think Maggie can help, though — she mentioned something about swimming practice. But I'll ask her." She raised her voice. "Maggie? Mrs. McCune's

6

sitter has been delayed. She needs somebody to stay with the twins for an hour or so until Mrs. Roman gets there."

"Can't," Maggie called from the kitchen. "We're practicing for the meet next Friday."

"No." Mrs. Butterman repeated the message. "And you know Ceci's away for the weekend. I'd be glad to help out myself, but I have a back-to-school exam to take in the — "

"Mom?" Peanut had come to stand beside her mother. "Mom!"

Mrs. Butterman stopped talking and looked down at her.

"Can I do it?" asked Peanut. "I've stayed with the twins when Mrs. McCune went grocery shopping."

"We-e-ell." Mrs. Butterman looked uncertain.

"She was gone for more than an hour when I stayed with the twins last week," Peanut went on. She really liked staying with Bridget and Deirdre. She liked being in charge.

Her mother spoke into the phone. "Polly is standing here at my elbow saying she'd like to help out. But I just don't know. . . . " She listened for a long time. "Yes, I can see you're in a fix."

Peanut held her breath.

"How long does Mrs. Roman think it will be before she gets there? . . . An hour, you say. Two at most? Mmmmmm."

"Mom!" Maggie hissed. She had come into the hall. "You can't let Peanut do that! She's too little!"

"I am not," Peanut said hotly.

"Are so," said Maggie. "I only started sitting this past summer."

"I'm more . . . more" — Peanut struggled for the right word — "more mature for my age than you are!"

"Ha!" said Maggie.

"Hush!" Mrs. Butterman held the phone against her shoulder. "I can't hear myself think. Mrs. McCune has a problem. Mr. McCune has already left. She's to meet him, and she can't get hold of him. She really does need someone desperately."

Peanut did her best to sound grown-up — mature. "I can do it. I know how to make

8

Bridget and Deirdre mind. And" — she had a sudden helpful thought — "Jilly can help, too. That will be two of us — one for each twin."

Mrs. Butterman made up her mind. "I think it will be all right," she said into the phone. "Polly says she'll bring Jilly with her. With the two of them there — "

"I'll call Jilly right away," Peanut promised. "Just to be sure. And, oh, is it okay if I bring Nibbsie with me? The twins like him. Ask her." She tugged at her mother's sleeve. "Ask her."

Mrs. Butterman asked. Still listening, she smiled and nodded at Peanut.

Peanut hugged herself. Then she hugged Nibbsie, which was better than hugging herself. "Hear that, Nibbs? It's okay for you to go, too."

Maggie looked disgusted and went back into the kitchen.

"I'm glad we can help," Mrs. Butterman said into the phone. "What are you seeing? *Swan Lake*? No wonder you don't want to miss it. Don't worry now — I'll see that she's there by eleven sharp."

9

She hung up the phone. "I hope I didn't promise more than you can deliver, my pet," she said. But she looked sure, sure that it would be okay for Peanut to be in charge. For an hour. Or two.

"You didn't promise too much," said Peanut. "You'll see. You'll just see."

Wait until Jilly heard. Oh, just wait. It was going to be fun to be in charge.

CHAPTER 2

Jilly's parents were going to Rockford today to deliver one of Mr. Matthews's jobs there. Mr. Matthews was an artist. He did work for many companies in and around Chicago. Jilly had been planning to go to Rockford with her father and mother and her little brother Jackie.

"It's only for an hour or two," Peanut went on. "Until Mrs. Roman gets there. Then we can take out our toboggan and try out the snow." She stretched the telephone cord almost to the front door, checking to see if the snow was still coming down. It was. "The twins are so cute," she added.

"Ha!" said Jilly. She had helped Peanut with Bridget and Deirdre before. "They're cute all right — when they're asleep," she joked. The twins looked like dainty little fairies. Except when they were acting like imps.

Peanut had to laugh. Bridget and Deirdre could be a handful. But she still found them fun. "There'll be two of us," she pointed out. "That's a twin apiece. What kind of mischief can they get into with both of us watching them?"

Jilly wavered. What Peanut said was true. The twins were small. She and Peanut were bigger. And smarter. "We-e-ell. . . ."

Peanut used her final argument. "I can't do it unless you'll come with me. That's what my mother said."

That did it. Peanut needed her. "Okay," said Jilly. "I'll go ask my mom."

She was away from the phone for ages. When she came back she was breathless. "It's okay. But we've got to promise not to let any strangers into the house. And Mrs. McCune is supposed to leave a list of numbers in case there's a big problem. And — "

"There won't be any problems," said Peanut. What kind of big problem could happen in a couple of hours, for heaven's sake? "Listen. I've got to be there by eleven o'clock. Come to my house and we'll go together."

She hung up, wondering whether parents went to Parents' School before they had children. At Parents' School they must learn how to say all the same things in exactly the same kind of voice. No cookies until you eat your carrots. Don't slam the door. Don't talk to strangers. Can you say "thank you," dear? She could think of dozens of things everybody's parents said.

Peanut had been dialing Mrs. McCune as she thought. The phone only rang twice. It was answered with a giggle and a thump as though it had been dropped. She could picture it lying on the floor with the twins — with their identical faces and identical curls and identical clothes — dancing around it. She could hear them.

"I'm talking on this telephone."

"No, you're not! I'm going to talk."

"I bet it's Grandma."

13

"If it's Grandma, she wants to talk to me more than to you."

"No. Me, me, me."

Peanut gulped a big breath. "Let me talk to your mother," she shouted in her loudest voice.

The background chatter stopped.

"Call your mommy to the telephone," she roared.

"Mommm-meeee!" The twins' voices faded as they moved away from the phone. "Some lady wants to talk to you."

Some *lady?* Never in her life had Peanut been called a lady!

"Hello?"

Mrs. McCune listened and was pleased to know that Jilly would indeed be coming to help Peanut. "You don't know what a lifesaver you are, Peanut. Besides which, you and Jilly are a lovely example for the girls. I hope," she added, sounding as though she didn't think it would really happen, "they will find best friends someday. Right now they aren't interested in anybody but each other."

Bark bark bark bark bark! Nibbsie was tired of waiting for Peanut. Bark. He had a right to his morning run. Bark bark. Hurry up, Peanut. Bark.

"Gotta go," Peanut said over the noise. "Tell the twins I'll bring Nibbsie with me, just like always."

Usually Nibbsie scampered ahead of Peanut. This morning, though, he wanted to run in circles, trying to catch all the white fluff that filled the air. The snow was glorious. It was coming down in big, fat, glompy clumps.

It's sticking, Peanut thought happily as she looked around at the snow-covered ground. It's not melting. With any luck, there would be lots of snow. She could help the twins make a snowman. Did they remember snow from last winter? Probably not. They were only three.

Her Saturday chores had to be done before she could go to the McCunes'. She went through the house like a whirlwind. It was her job to empty all the wastebaskets and to dust everything in the living room. That meant dusting all the books on the shelves — and not just a swipe across the tops, either. She had to take them off the shelves one by one, wipe them off, and put them back.

15

She was nearly finished when Mrs. Butterman came downstairs dressed to go out, wearing her nicest blazer and plaid skirt and her boots. "You won't be able to call me, of course," she said. "But I should be home by five. Oh, I wish Poppy and Nonny were here. I'd feel better about going away on a Saturday if they were home."

Was her mother ever going to stop treating her like a baby? It was a very big burden for Peanut to bear. She almost said something about that. Then she saw the worried frown on her mother's face, and instead she said, "You can give me their phone number down in Florida if you like. I'll call them and tell them they're missing the first snowstorm."

"Silly!" Mrs. Butterman had to laugh. "You know what I mean. I'd feel better if there was someone to call in an emergency."

The doorbell rang. That had to be Jilly.

Mrs. Butterman pulled on her gloves and gave Peanut a quick peck on the cheek. "Indulge your little old mother," she said. "I can't help being concerned over my baby."

Thank goodness she said that before she

called good-bye up the stairway to Maggie and let Jilly in.

"Ready?" asked Jilly. "Set?"

"Go!" said Peanut. "Come on, Nibbsie," she called. "Or I'll go without you."

When they got to the McCunes', the twins were waiting at the front windows, their noses pressed against the glass, laughing. Peanut picked up two big handfuls of snow and pressed it against the glass, right over their faces. Bridget and Deirdre ran shrieking. The sound cut through the glass and brick.

"Do all little kids screech like that?" asked Jilly.

"I'm sure I never did," said Peanut.

"Me, neither," said Jilly. "I'm sure I'd remember if I did."

CHAPTER
3

The twins hopped around, reaching for Nibbsie, when Mrs. McCune opened the door. Peanut held him safely against her shoulder. "Nibbsie's only a little dog," she said. "He's afraid of you. You have to treat him gently."

The twins looked awed. The little dog was afraid of them? Imagine!

"I'll hold him," said Peanut. She did this each time she came to the McCunes'. "You pet him." She leaned down.

The little hands stroked Nibbsie's furry back and head.

19

"Not his nose," said Peanut, "or his eyes. He wouldn't like that."

Mrs. McCune closed the door behind Peanut and Jilly. "I don't know what I'd have done if you couldn't come. I've had ballet tickets for weeks and I'd have simply expired if I'd had to cancel. I mean, I'd have died." She was glowing with excitement.

Mrs. McCune was pretty old. She had told Peanut she was twenty-four. But sometimes she sounded more like one of Peanut's friends than an adult. Usually she dressed the way they did, too, in jeans and a sweatshirt. Today she looked very grown-up. She had on a pale yellow dress with a full, swingy skirt. She was wearing makeup and earrings that were probably real pearls.

Peanut set Nibbsie down. He had to look after himself now. If the twins got rough, he would outrun them. Or he'd bark and scare them. Or he'd come running to Peanut.

"I've fixed this month's favorite lunch," said Mrs. McCune, leading the way into the kitchen. "Last month all we wanted was macaroni and cheese. Two weeks ago we discovered hot dogs and beans."

She showed them where things in the kitchen were kept. And she went over the list of important numbers hanging beside the phone — a doctor's name, and St. Francis Hospital, and the fire and police departments. "You won't need them, of course," she said. "But it's good to know the phone numbers are there."

She bustled around the kitchen, chattering about how she was going to meet Mr. Mc-Cune — Malachy, she called him — in the Loop. He had gone to his office to get some quiet-time work done. They were going to have lunch at the Art Institute. And then they were going to see a ballet, *Swan Lake*. And she could hardly wait.

Mrs. McCune served up the hot dogs and beans on Little Miss Muffet plates. "I hope you girls like hot dogs and beans. There's plenty here. Will you put the twins' cover-ups on them?"

Peanut found the denim cover-ups hanging on low, child-high hooks behind the kitchen

21

door. "One for you and one for me," she said softly, handing one to Jilly. She reached for the nearest twin. "Come on, Deirdre. It's lunch-time."

"I'm not Deirdre." The little girl's lip stuck out. "I'm Bridget."

"Gotcha!" said Peanut. She was ready for this. It was another thing they went through each time she came here. The little girls insisted on not being mixed up. She dug out the safety pin she had ready in her pocket. "Bridget," she said firmly, fastening the pin to Bridget's collar. "I'm not going to forget you, Bridget. Hear that, Jilly?" she asked. "That's Deirdre you've got there. She's the one without the safety pin."

"Lunchtime," said Jilly, swinging Deirdre up into her chair. "How about some beans and a hot dog?"

Mrs. McCune disappeared into the hall.

"And apple sauce?" said Jilly, spotting it in a bowl beside the sink.

"And a cookie?" asked Deirdre.

"After lunch," said Peanut, who knew all about having to wait for cookies until plates had been cleaned off. She wrapped Bridget's fingers around her spoon. "Beans," she said. "Yummy."

"Yummy," said Bridget.

"I think we're supposed to cut up their hot dogs," said Jilly, who knew something about the way small children eat. She had seen her mother cut up Jackie's food a million times.

Peanut found a table knife and cut up the hot dogs into bite-size pieces.

Mrs. McCune came back into the kitchen wearing her coat. "Who's got a kiss for Mommy?" she asked.

Bridget and Deirdre were more interested in hot dogs than kisses. Their eyes fixed on their plates, they tilted their cheeks to be kissed.

"I'm glad they're not fussing," Mrs. McCune said softly over their heads. "I'm sure they'll be just fine with you until Mrs. Roman gets here. She may even make it before you've finished lunch. If she doesn't, pop the girls into bed for their naps right after lunch. Tell Mrs. Roman I'll call during the afternoon."

Peanut had a last question. "When the twins

wake up from their naps, may we take them out into the backyard and help them make a snowman?"

Mrs. McCune glanced at the window and the swirling whiteness beyond. "What fun! It'll be their first snowman. But don't keep them out too long. If they're soaked when you come inside, tell Mrs. Roman to dunk them in a warm tub. Oh, why am I fussing?" she said, almost to herself. "Mrs. Roman knows what to do!"

With a last glance at the twins, she was gone.

And Peanut was finally in charge. She felt like . . . like . . . Was this the way a king or queen or a president of a country felt? In charge of everything? "We've got to keep our strength up," she said. "Let's have a hot dog."

She found bread and butter and Jilly poured milk for everybody. They settled down at the table on either side of the twins.

Peanut wrapped her hot dog in a slice of bread. With mustard. And ketchup. And pickle relish. Yummy good. She opened her mouth to take a bite.

"All done," said a small voice.

"But you've still got some beans there," said Peanut, pointing at Bridget's plate.

"Not hungry," said Bridget.

Jilly had at least gotten to eat one bite of her hot dog. She swallowed. "Try some beans," she said, offering a spoonful to Deirdre. "Ummmm. Good."

The twins each picked up a bean, a single bean, and bit it in half.

"All done," they said in a single voice, returning the uneaten half beans to their plates.

Peanut looked longingly at her hot dog. Weren't she and Jilly going to have time to eat anything? Maybe if she helped. . . .

She took Bridget's spoon, dipped it into the Miss Muffet plate, and offered it — just as the little girl rocked forward in her chair. The beans connected with the top of her head.

Bridget put a hand on her head and came away with a handful of beans. She popped them into her mouth.

"Oh, gag!" Peanut covered her eyes. It was going to be one of those afternoons.

"Cats get hairballs from licking them-

25

selves," Jilly said thoughtfully. "Do you suppose little kids get hairballs if they eat food out of their hair?"

Now *that* was a thought Peanut didn't want to have. She would worry about it later. She got a wet paper towel and cleaned the beans out of Bridget's hair and off her fingers.

"Beans are beads," said Deirdre. One by one she lined up beans into a necklace on the table around her plate.

Jilly watched, fascinated.

"Hurry up and eat," Peanut muttered to Jilly. They might not have time to eat for the rest of the afternoon. "While they're busy." She leaned down and gave a piece of hot dog to Nibbsie, who was sitting up, begging.

"Are we supposed to make them eat everything on their plates?" Jilly asked between mouthfuls.

"Don't know what we can do if they won't," said Peanut. She did some more cleaning up with wet towels and gave the twins their cookies. "I don't think their teeth will fall out or their hair will come uncurled in just one afternoon." She remembered hearing about teeth and curly hair when she was small and refused to eat lunch.

She also remembered hearing about not eating fast. But she gulped down her hot dog. "Come on," she said, "let's clean them up and get them into bed for their naps."

That was easier said than done. They used tons of paper towels and wet washcloths to clean up the wiggling twins, who had decided they didn't want to take a nap.

"Not sleepy."

"Don't want a nap."

"But I'm going to read to you," Jilly promised.

"And I'm going to sing to you," said Peanut.

Jilly read *The Three Little Pigs*. She was pretty good at huffing and puffing and blowing pigs' houses down. Bridget and Deirdre loved it.

Peanut read *Goldilocks*. It was a quieter story.

The twins' thumbs went into their mouths.

Peanut knew they shouldn't be sucking their thumbs. But for this one afternoon — why not?

Then she and Jilly took turns reciting, more

and more slowly, all the Mother Goose rhymes they could think of.

The twins yawned around their thumbs. Their eyes opened and closed, opened and closed . . . opened . . . closed . . . and stayed shut.

Peanut and Jilly tiptoed out of the bedroom. They had just enough time to clean up the kitchen before the twins woke up.

CHAPTER 4

Peanut scrubbed at the kitchen table. She had already cleaned beans off the floor and the chairs. "Bridget and Deirdre sure are messy. I just know I was never this messy."

"What'll I do with the beans in this pan?" Jilly asked from the stove.

Peanut wasn't sure. "Just put them in the fridge. Maybe Mrs. McCune can feed them to the twins tomorrow."

Jilly made room for the pan of beans in the refrigerator. "There's orange juice in here," she said over her shoulder.

"Let's have some," said Peanut. "Mrs. McCune

always tells me I can drink anything in there."

She found glasses, and Jilly poured the juice.

A sound came from overhead. A thunk. Something dropped.

Startled, Peanut looked toward the ceiling. Nibbsie barked and shot out of the kitchen, heading toward the stairs. Peanut and Jilly raced after him.

A giggle came from the bedroom at the front of the house. What was going on? Warily Peanut and Jilly tiptoed along the hallway and peeked in.

The twins were standing on the bench in front of Mrs. McCune's fluffy-skirted dressing table, leaning close to the mirror, looking at themselves. The faces they turned to Peanut and Jilly were covered with lipstick. And powder. And blusher. And eye makeup.

"Pickle juice!" Jilly breathed in awe.

Peanut sagged against the door frame. The little faces were a mess, a ghastly mess.

"I'm a pretty lady," said Bridget, she of the safety pin.

"Me, too," chortled Deirdre.

"You're not supposed to mess around in your

mom's makeup," Peanut wailed. "That's only for big ladies."

"I'm big," the twins insisted in one voice. They climbed down from the bench and picked up their dolls to prove it.

"Mommy showed me I'm bigger than Chryssy."

"She showed me I'm lots bigger than Missy."

"But you're lots smaller than me," said Peanut. "And if you're smaller than I am, you aren't supposed to wear makeup."

Jilly groaned. "Look at what they did to the mirror." It was covered with lipstick stick men and scribbles and smears.

But the mirror wasn't what caught Peanut's eye. Nibbsie was sniffing at a cologne bottle lying on its side on the floor, the stopper next to it. She picked up the bottle. Empty. It was empty. Her heart stopped. Where was the cologne, if it wasn't in the bottle? It wasn't inside Bridget and Deirdre, was it? Oh, they hadn't drunk it! Or — had they?

She held up the bottle. "What did you do with this?" she demanded. She was scared and she sounded stern, as stern as any grown-up.

The little girls' eyes were round and frightened.

Peanut knelt down, smiling, sniffing at the bottle. "Mmm-mmm. Smells good," she said softly.

The twins' heads pumped up and down. They agreed. It smelled wonderful.

"But it's a-a-all gone." Peanut sang the words. "Where did it go?"

"In the toilet," said Bridget.

"Mommy says it's toilet water," said Deirdre.

"So we put it there," said Bridget.

There was a moment of silence as Peanut and Jilly took in what they had just heard. Then they threw back their heads and hooted with laughter.

"I don't believe it," gasped Peanut.

"I'll check," said Jilly, running out of the bedroom. A moment later she called from the bathroom. "That's what they did, all right. The water's pink." She came back into the bedroom. "Wait'll I tell my mom!"

Peanut stopped laughing. "I think we're not supposed to encourage them."

Bridget and Deirdre were huddled together. Puzzlement was written on their faces over, under, and around the streaks of makeup.

Peanut tried to explain. "I don't know why it's called toilet water. But it's perfume. You're supposed to put it behind your ears so you smell good."

Jilly had stopped laughing. "How're we going to get that stuff off their faces? Should we use dish soap? Or . . . or . . . Comet?"

"I don't think you're supposed to use those on people," said Peanut. She remembered watching Ceci take off her makeup. "I bet there's some face cream here." She poked around among the clutter on the dressing table and held up a jar. "Here. Let's try this."

The little girls stood still and let their faces be creamed. Then they wanted to look at themselves in the mirror.

"Now off it comes," said Peanut, scrubbing at the lipstick that covered half of — which twin's face? She checked for the safety pin. It wasn't there. So this was Deirdre's face she was scrubbing.

"Don't want to. Don't want to," wailed Deirdre, trying to break free. "Want to be a pretty lady."

Peanut had her locked between her knees and kept right on rubbing. "You want to go outdoors and make a snowman, don't you?"

Deirdre's eyes popped open. She was still.

Peanut pointed toward the window. "That's snow out there. After you finish your nap, we're going to go outside and play in the snow. Do you want to help make a snowman?"

Deirdre's lips tilted upward. She bobbed her head and kept on bobbing it — which made it hard not to scrub the cream and makeup into her hair. Peanut sighed.

"But first," she went on, "you've got to get the pretty lady stuff off your face and hands. And then you've got to finish your nap so you'll be big and strong enough to make a" — she sang the words — "Frosty, the Snowman."

Deirdre had nothing more to say. She stopped wiggling, and Peanut finished cleaning her up and putting her into clean clothes.

"You're really wonderful," said Jilly. "It

36

worked. What's-her-face here is cooperating, too."

They tucked the twins in and Peanut sang "Frosty the Snowman" softly and more softly until they were asleep. Again. They really were tired. They really did need their naps.

"Like I said," said Jilly, "they're cute when they're *asleep*. But do you trust them to stay asleep?"

"Not on your life!" said Peanut. "We're going to stay upstairs until Mrs. Roman comes. Come on — let's clean up the dressing table."

"Do you use cleansing cream on that, too?" asked Jilly.

They wiped up the spilled powder with tissues. But the mirror — that was another matter. Maybe cleansing cream was worth trying. . . .

"I don't think this mirror is ever going to be shiny again," Peanut said, giving it a last good rub. "Maybe Mrs. Roman will know how to get it clean."

Jilly waited on the top step while Peanut went downstairs and got magazines and their orange juice and filled a water bowl in the kitchen for Nibbsie. They spent the next hour sitting on the steps.

After a while it became hard to see the words in the magazines. The house was dark, even though it was afternoon.

"The snow is really coming down hard," said Peanut, turning on the hall lamp. "Maybe we'll have a blizzard." She said it hopefully.

"Wouldn't that be neat!" said Jilly. "How much snow makes a blizzard? I mean, what's the difference between a plain snowstorm and a blizzard?"

Peanut wasn't sure. But she wished it would happen. Evanston would be a perfect place to live if there were only a blizzard now and then. Not even a huge blizzard. Just a sort of medium one. Her wishes were interrupted by the telephone.

She answered it on the extension in the front bedroom. "McCune residence. Polly Butterm — "

"Polly! My dear!" The voice at the other end of the line was breathless. "This is Catherine

Roman. I know I promised Mrs. McCune I'd be there by now, but I'm still out here at Old Orchard. My glasses are fixed. But the weather has turned simply frightful."

It was the nicest news Peanut had heard in weeks.

"The snow is heavy. My car is stuck."

Peanut smiled, thinking how much snow it took to get a car "stuck."

"Public transportation has slowed to a crawl."

That must mean a blizzard! How wonderful! How simply great!

"Honestly, I'm worried about you there, all by yourself. But I don't know what I can do about it."

Peanut was grinning. "Don't worry, Mrs. Roman," she said kindly. "Everything here is under control. Just enjoy the snow."

"What? What did you say? Oh. Enjoy the snow. Oh, I can't really enjoy it, knowing I should be there with you."

What could Peanut say so that Mrs. Roman could enjoy the snow? "The twins are taking their nap," she said soothingly. "My friend

Jilly is here. Don't worry. Whenever you get here, we'll be waiting for you. Everything will be just fine."

"Yes. Well, I'll do my best," said Mrs. Roman. "I'll get there eventually. You can count on it. Good-bye, dear."

"Mrs. Roman?" Peanut called. She had suddenly remembered something. "How do you get makeup off a — ?"

Click. The phone went dead. The un-shiny mirror would have to stay that way until Mrs. Roman got there.

But — a blizzard was going on. Fantastic! Awesome — simply awesome!

CHAPTER
5

A lot of snow had fallen since morning. Peanut was surprised by how deep it was. It had blown into drifts against the fence, against the garage, against the back of the house. It swirled and swooped in the wind.

In their yellow snowsuits, the twins were bright spots of color in the grayness. They stood in wonder, watching as the snow turned into droplets of water on their mittens. They hadn't moved since Peanut and Jilly set them down when they came out into the backyard.

"I don't think they *can* move," said Jilly,

watching them. "The snow is practically up to their shoulders."

"Come on," said Peanut. "Let's fix a place where they can play."

They trampled and stomped the snow, walking in circles. The twins stomped after them, falling down and shrieking in delight. Since they were lying down in the snow anyway, Jilly showed them how to make snow angels. Soon the play space was surrounded by small shadowy angels in the snow.

Peanut tested a handful of snow. It packed nicely. "Hey, Jilly," she yelled.

Jilly turned. The snowball smacked into her face. "You rat!" she screamed, spitting out snow and wiping off her face. "You dirty rat!" She scooped up snow and threw it. It missed Peanut by a mile.

The twins were forgotten.

Just as Peanut was ready to let loose another snowball, Jilly yelled, "Hi, Mrs. McCune. Aren't you home early?"

Peanut turned to look. Jilly's snowball caught her in the neck and slid down inside her jacket.

"EEE-yiiii!" she screamed. "That's cold. Now who's a rat?"

Bridget and Deirdre had been watching. They thought they knew how to play this game. "You rat!" they yelled, tossing snow wildly. "You dirty rat."

Peanut and Jilly stopped in mid-throw. Their arms dropped to their sides.

"I don't think we'd better say that R-word anymore," said Peanut.

"They're copy machines," said Jilly. "They do whatever we do."

"Snowman coming up," said Peanut. "Hey, kids. Watch what I'm going to do with *this* snowball." She began rolling it along the ground.

The twins, copycats, tried doing the same thing.

Peanut's snowball got bigger and bigger. Jilly came to help her push it. When it was so big they couldn't move it another inch, they left it standing where it stopped and began packing snow onto it, building it taller, taller.

The twins helped, stretching as high as they could.

It was, finally, a pretty good snowman, almost as tall as a grown-up. But it didn't have a face.

"In storybooks, people make a mouth and eyes out of coal," said Peanut. "Have you ever seen coal? I haven't."

Jilly hadn't, either. "I asked my father once, and he said it's kind of like charcoal. People used to burn it for heat before there was gas and electricity."

"I'll bet there's a carrot for a nose in the kitchen," said Peanut. "I'll go see what I can find. Don't take your eyes off the twins," she warned.

"See if you can find a hat," Jilly called after her. "And a scarf."

The wind blew away her words. Peanut could hardly hear her.

Inside the house, she went to the refrigerator. Would Mrs. McCune mind? Well, it was, after all, the twins' first snowman. . . .

She found a carrot in the vegetable crisper. Good. But — what else could she use?

Then she remembered something. Mrs.

McCune made ice-cube pops for the twins, frozen cranberry juice on sticks. Surely she wouldn't mind some of those for a snowman. They might even stay frozen, and the twins could eat them later.

She found them and put them into a pan. On her way outside, she grabbed one of the red towels from the rack — a good scarf. She would go outdoors and get it before she left that afternoon.

"Ice pops!" shrieked Deirdre when she saw what Peanut had in the pan.

"Want an ice pop." Bridget jumped up and down.

They danced around Peanut, reaching, reaching.

Peanut held the pan above their heads. "Oh, you don't want these. These are for the snowman's face. After he has a face we're going indoors and we're having hot chocolate."

Bridget and Deirdre didn't look as though they thought that was a good trade for ice pops.

"With marshmallows," said Jilly.

"Six marshmallows," said Deirdre. "Or three?" She wasn't sure which was the bigger number.

"Two great big ones," said Peanut, pressing the ice pops into a smile on the snowman's face. The sticks made them stay in place.

"That's a great face," said Jilly. "Hey — you can use the pan for a hat."

Peanut put it on the snowman's head and added the red kitchen towel. "Frosty the Snowman," she said, standing back.

The twins cocked their heads, looking up at the snowman. Their cheeks were scarlet. Suddenly Peanut remembered what Mrs. McCune had said about not keeping them out in the cold too long. "Time to go in," she said.

"No!" the twins protested. "No."

"Oh, I can almost smell that chocolate," said Jilly.

"With two sweet, gooey marshmallows," said Peanut. "And we'll be all toasty warm and sit by the window and look at our snowman."

The marshmallows did it. Looking back over their shoulders at the snowman, the little girls permitted themselves to be pulled indoors.

"How did they get so wet?" Jilly asked in wonder as they unzipped and unbuttoned the twins. They were soaked to the skin. "I mean, I played in the snow, too, but just my mittens and socks are wet."

Free of their snowsuits, the twins raced to the kitchen window to look at the snowman.

"I think we'd better get them warm and dry before they have hot chocolate," said Peanut, watching them.

And so it was back upstairs. Back into the bathroom. Into and out of a warm bubble bath. Into dry underclothes and socks.

Jilly had an idea. "It would be easy to tell them apart if they weren't always dressed exactly alike."

Now that Peanut thought about it, why *did* Mrs. McCune always dress Bridget and Deirdre in matching clothes? "If they were dressed in different colors, we wouldn't have to put a safety pin on Bridget's collar. We'd know which twin was which."

She found yellow corduroy pants and a matching sweatshirt in the closet. "Isn't this neat?" she asked, holding up the sweatshirt. "It's even got a hood. I'd like it myself — if it was ninety sizes bigger."

Jilly found a skirt with tulips on it and a tulip shirt to match. She pulled Deirdre close and struggled to get her arms into the sleeves.

"This is kind of like dressing dolls," said Peanut, trying to figure out how to get the shirt over Bridget's head. It *was* Bridget — Peanut had tested — and she definitely did not like things pulled over her head. "Except that dolls don't fight you," said Peanut, tugging. Bridget fought. At last her head popped through the sweatshirt.

Peanut patted everything into place and turned her around so that Jilly could see.

Jilly gave a last tug to Deirdre's dress and turned her to face Peanut.

The little girls looked at each other. Their mouths opened round. They pointed at each other.

"She's prettier than me," wailed Bridget.

"She's prettier," sobbed Deirdre. "Prettier."

"Hold it," Peanut said hastily. "Nobody's

prettier than anybody. Do you want to change, or shall I?" she asked Jilly.

"I will," said Jilly. "It's maybe easier to get Deirdre out of this than it is to get Bridget out of that."

"Well," said Peanut as Jilly made the switch, "I guess we figured out why Mrs. McCune dresses them alike."

Sunshine and smiles returned when the twins found themselves dressed in matching outfits. They followed Peanut back downstairs and pressed their noses to the window, looking at the snowman. Jilly made the hot chocolate. Peanut hunted for marshmallows in the pantry.

"There's so much snow coming down I can hardly see the snowman," said Jilly as she filled mugs with the hot chocolate.

"Wouldn't it be great to have our hot chocolate in front of the fireplace?" asked Peanut. "But I don't think I'd better start a fire."

"Anyway," said Jilly, "if we took the hot chocolate into the living room, how much do you want to bet it would end up on the floor?"

"Let's not!" said Peanut. "Oh, let's not!"

They stayed in the kitchen to drink their hot chocolate — with two marshmallows. They helped Bridget and Deirdre so that the yellow outfits stayed yellow without chocolate spots. If there was anything they didn't need, it was another change of clothes.

CHAPTER
6

Peanut loved old movies. But it was hard to
enjoy Fred Astaire and Ginger Rogers today.
Because the phone kept ringing. Because the
twins kept wiggling around on the sofa, their
heads bobbing up in front of the TV screen.

She solved the wiggling part by setting the
little girls on the floor, well away from the
TV, with coloring books and crayons. "Color a
pretty picture for me," she said.

Bridget and Deirdre scribbled.

"Come show your pictures to Jilly when you
finish," Jilly said over her shoulder, one eye

on the TV. This movie was too good to miss even one minute of it.

"Isn't Ginger Rogers wonderful?" said Peanut, coming back to the sofa. Ginger tapped her way up a curving white stairway and back down, following Fred all the way. "She almost makes me want to learn to dance."

The telephone jangled, and she went to answer it.

It was Mrs. McCune. "Peanut — you're still there! How nice for the girls. But let me talk to Mrs. Roman."

Oh, how Peanut at that moment wished she could let Mrs. McCune talk to Mrs. Roman. "Uh," she said, "uh — Mrs. Roman hasn't come yet."

A gasp came over the line.

"But she's on her way," Peanut added hastily. "She called and said she would be late, but she's coming and I could count on it. And everything is just fine. The twins are coloring in their coloring books."

"Oh, dear." The peppiness had gone out of Mrs. McCune's voice. "It's intermission. I think we'll leave right now."

But how terrible not to see the rest of *Swan Lake*. "Honestly, Bridget and Deirdre are fine," said Peanut. "And maybe Mrs. Roman will get here any minute. And then you'll have missed half the ballet for nothing."

There was a long pause. Voices muttered. Peanut couldn't hear what they were saying. At last Mrs. McCune came back onto the line. "I just talked with my husband. You're sure everything is all right?"

"It couldn't be better," said Peanut.

"Mr. McCune says that since it will only be another hour or so, we will stay for the rest of the performance and then we'll race right home. Now you're sure you're all right?"

"Absolutely," said Peanut. "Positively. Sure. Certainly. Yes, *ma'am!*"

Mrs. McCune laughed. It wasn't her usual lighthearted laugh, but it was an improvement over the way she had been sounding. "All right, then. I'll call before we leave, and it shouldn't take us long after that." A bell sounded in the background. "There's the curtain bell. I'll talk to you in an hour or so, then. Kiss the girls for me."

Peanut replaced the phone and, stepping around Bridget and Deirdre, went back to Fred and Ginger. Ginger was leaning far back over Fred's arm, looking up into his eyes as they danced. "Everything he does she does backward," she said. "I wonder if that's harder than dancing forward."

"Those old-time ways of fixing hair sure were weird," said Jilly. "Her hair looks so stiff. But she's pretty anyway."

"My grandma saw her once in person," said Peanut. She had a funny thought. "I wonder if she's as old as Nonny." What a strange idea — the beautiful girl on the TV screen, old, like Nonny.

The phone rang again. Peanut let it ring for a minute, walking backward, her eyes on the TV, watching the end of a dance number. "McCune residence," she said finally, picking up the phone. "Polly Butterman speaking."

"Oh, Peanut." It was Mrs. Matthews. "Is everything all right there?"

Why did people keep thinking things wouldn't be all right? Peanut told her how super-dandy

55

everything was. "We're watching TV," she added.

"Good," said Mrs. Matthews. "I just wanted you to know we might be a bit late getting back. The snow out here west of Chicago is heavy. Is Jilly nearby? I'd like to talk to her."

Peanut and Jilly traded places at the phone, and Peanut got to watch more of Ginger and Fred. She could almost feel herself floating the way Ginger seemed to, with a dress swishing around her in that glamorous way.

"My mom says the Interstate is a mess and the driving is slow," said Jilly, plopping down on the sofa beside Peanut. She curled up, her eyes on the movie. Ginger and Fred were walking — not dancing — down a street filled with old-time cars. "Isn't her dress funny? It's not really long, but it's not short, either."

"I like hoop skirts better," said Peanut. "But I bet it was hard to ride a bike in them."

"Did this movie happen before or after miniskirts?" asked Jilly.

They didn't know.

The movie broke for a commercial. Jilly

stretched and yawned. "You haven't shown me your pretty pictures yet," she said over her shoulder to the twins.

Peanut turned to look. The coloring books and crayons lay scattered. The little girls were nowhere to be seen. "Bridget?" she called. "Deirdre?"

There was no answer.

"Oh, my gosh," she moaned, leaping to her feet. "They're gone." She flew toward the kitchen. Maybe they were looking out the window at the snowman.

"How did they get away without us knowing it?" asked Jilly, running after her. "We were right there all the time."

Except for Nibbsie, asleep under the table, the kitchen was empty. So was the back hall.

Peanut's heart dropped down into her shoes. She ran back the way she had come, checking the dining room, the den. Nobody. She stopped in the front hall. This was thinking time. . . .

The twins were in the house somewhere. The question was — where? And what were they doing? The thing about the twins was, you had to act like you were in charge. "I'm coming," she called in a isn't-this-a-fun-game voice. "Ready or not."

A giggle exploded from upstairs. That's where they were.

She bounded up the steps two at a time, Jilly close behind her. At the top of the stairs, she stopped dead still, staring at the carpeting outside the bathroom. It was covered with small, white footprints. She tiptoed to the door and looked in.

The two halves of a bath powder box lay upside down beside the tub. Powder covered the pink tile floor. The twins — powdery white from their curls to their toes — knelt in the middle of the mess, patting it, stirring it, having a perfectly lovely time.

"Inside snow," Bridget explained, looking up at Peanut.

"We're making snowballs," said Deirdre.

They flung handfuls of it at each other.

"You rat," said Deirdre.

"You dirty rat," said Bridget.

They laughed gleefully.

Peanut and Jilly turned sick smiles on each

other. Never in the whole history of Evanston, in the whole history of baby-sitting, had there been such a mess.

The twins had become quiet under Peanut's horrified gaze. They stuck their thumbs in their mouths and lifted their free hands to twirl at locks of their hair.

"Hold it!" gasped Peanut, grabbing the nearest thumb. "Don't eat it! Don't put it in your mouth. Or your hair!"

Jilly dived for the other twin. "We've got to get them out of these clothes in here," she said, "so they don't track the stuff around the rest of the house."

They stripped off the yellow outfits, setting up a blizzard of powder, and rubbed the little girls with bath towels. Happily, the towels were white. The powder didn't show on them.

Jilly leaned back and inspected her twin. "How'll we get the stuff out of their hair?"

"Brush it, I guess," said Peanut. "I don't think we ought to try washing their hair."

Jilly remembered Jackie screeching at having his hair washed, rubbing soapy water into his eyes, struggling to get away. She shud-

dered. "We will *not* wash their hair," she said
firmly.

"Tell you what," said Peanut. "Suppose we
take them into their room and shut the door
so they can't get out. I'll get some towels.
Maybe rubbing their hair will help. You can
put clean clothes on them. And I'll — ugh! —
clean up the bathroom."

The bathroom was certainly the worst of the
two jobs. And it was her responsibility. Jilly
was only acting like a true friend in being
here at all.

Wiping their feet on the used towels and
stepping clear of the bathroom doorsill, they
lugged the squirming twins to their bedroom
and dumped them on their beds.

Oh goody! A new game! The little girls
squealed and began to bounce. Thoink
. . . thoink . . . thoink. . . .

Peanut darted to the hall linen closet, grabbed
towels, and took them back to the bedroom.
She tossed them inside and stood with her
head through the partly open door, ready to
get out of there. "I hope you know you've got
the easiest job," she said.

"Easy!" groaned Jilly, poking around in the chest of drawers. She held up a brush. "I've got to get the powder out of their hair."

"Want to trade? Want to clean up the bathroom?"

"Not on your life!"

"Congratulate yourself on your luck."

"I'm congratulating. I'm congratulating."

They grinned at each other and Peanut ducked out, closing the door firmly.

She went to stand outside the bathroom. What a mess!

Thoink . . . thoink . . . thoink . . . giggle . . . shriek. The twins were having fun, and maybe Jilly was, too. But here she was, by herself, a cleanup crew of one. No fun.

How was she going to get all that powder off the floor?

Being in charge was great when things were fine. It was terrible when things were rotten.

Thoink . . . giggle. . . .

But it had to be done.

Shriek . . . thoink . . . thoink. . . .

Peanut pulled her shoulders back. "Now see here, Peanut Butterman," she said to herself.

"Being in charge means something special. You .. are .. going .. to .. figure .. out .. what .. to .. do."

What was there to work with? Not a broom — that would only stir up clouds of powder. A washcloth might work if it was good and wet. Hey — what she needed was a sponge mop.

She raced downstairs, found a mop, filled a pail, and returned to the scene of the crime. Working carefully, she pushed the wet mop into the room from the doorway. It made a shiny, powder-free path.

She dipped the mop into the pail, made more shiny paths, and began to feel wonderfully smart. The powder was coming off the floor. Yes, sir, all right! Peanut Butterman was in charge, and Peanut Butterman could take care of problems, no matter what they were.

She began to sing. " 'Heigh ho, heigh ho, it's off to work we go' — "

Bong! The doorbell sounded.

Who could that be? It certainly wasn't the McCunes. They couldn't be home so soon. Maybe it was Mrs. Roman.

Bong!

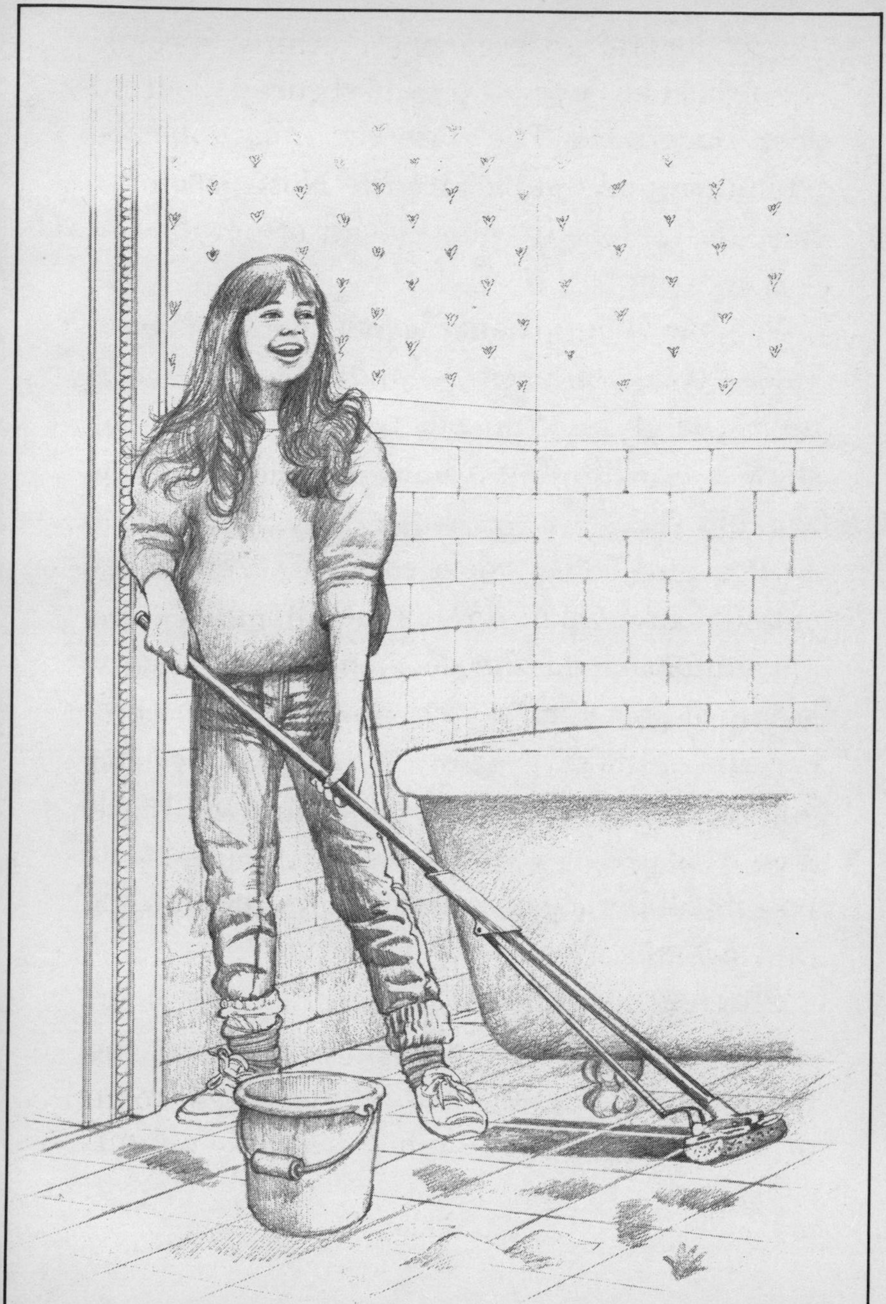

Nibbsie started barking.

She dashed downstairs and checked the front door. Bong-bong! The glass was almost blocked by snow piled against it. She didn't even try to open it. Nobody could be out there.

Bong-bong!

The back door, then. She dashed to the back hall — bong-bong-bong — and put her face right up to the glass. Who was that out there? The snow was whipping around in the wind. She couldn't see.

"Pea-nut!" The voice carried through the closed door. "Open up. It's me, Maggie."

Peanut tugged the door open, and Maggie stumped past her, setting down a plastic grocery bag, shaking snow off in all directions, wiping snow off her face. "Just thought I'd stop in to see how things are going," she said, pulling off her cap, two scarves, mittens, jacket, and sweater. "I came on my skis."

She reached out and rubbed Peanut's head, and then hopped around on one foot, tugging off her boots. Gone was the unhappy Maggie of the morning. "I brought some brownie mix from home. I thought it would be fun to make brownies."

Brownies? But brownies were fattening. Why was Maggie going to feed her brownies?

Maggie saw her wonderment. "Aw, look, Little Bit." She hadn't called Peanut Little Bit in so long that Peanut had almost forgotten her baby nickname. "I'm really sorry about this morning. Mom gave me the business. She said I'm unhappy about not being in Minneapolis and I was taking it out on you. So I'm sorry. And I won't do that anymore. Okay?"

She put her hands on Peanut's shoulders, looking into her eyes. She smiled as only Maggie could — as though there were a thousand-watt light bulb inside her. Nobody could stay mad at Maggie when she smiled like that. "Okay?"

"Okay," Peanut agreed. Maggie could be a really neat sister sometimes.

Maggie's eyes strayed down to Peanut's powdery sweatshirt. "My gosh! What happened to you?"

Peanut told about the bath powder snowball fight. She couldn't help making a funny story of it — it really was funny, when she thought about it. "I'm cleaning up the bathroom," she finished.

Maggie groaned. "I'll help," she offered, "before we do the brownies." She followed Peanut upstairs and stopped outside the bathroom, taking in the powdery footprints, the powdery pink floor. "Wow! Oh wow!"

"It's beginning to look good," said Peanut. "You should've seen it a while ago."

"Just tell me what to do," said Maggie.

She, Peanut? Give orders to Maggie? How weird! Never in her whole life had she told Maggie what to do! But suddenly Peanut did know what to say. "Want to get the vacuum cleaner?" she asked. "You can clean up the carpet while I finish in the bathroom."

"Yes, sir, Sarge," said Maggie, snapping a salute.

Together, Peanut and Maggie finished cleaning up the bath powder blitz.

A crew of two was better any old day than a crew of one. . . .

66

CHAPTER
7

Peanut had her hands full just answering the telephone.

Mrs. Butterman called. She had called home, and since Peanut wasn't there she had guessed she was still at the McCunes'. She was getting ready to leave. Someone said it was blizzarding outside. Peanut wasn't to worry. The trains always ran. She would be there soon.

Mrs. McCune called. They were at the parking garage waiting for their car to be brought down. Mrs. Roman still hadn't come? But Maggie was there? Oh, she was so glad Maggie was there, just in case.

In case of what? Really! It was practically insulting that Mrs. McCune thought everything was better because Maggie had come!

Now, Peanut wasn't to worry. There was snow, true. But the snowplows would be out. The Outer Drive was always kept open. They would be home soon.

Mrs. Gilman called. Mrs. Gilman lived next door. Mr. and Mrs. McCune weren't home? Oh, dear! Polly was the baby-sitter! Dear me! Dear-dear-dear! If there were any problems, Polly was to call. Write down the number, dear. Polly wasn't to worry. The Gilmans were right there, right next door. They could come in a minute if Polly needed them. Now, don't worry, dear.

A man selling magazine subscriptions called. He didn't tell Peanut not to worry.

Why did everybody think she would worry? What was there to worry about? The snow was outside. Inside, it was warm and cozy. The worst thing that could happen was that the house would be buried in a giant snow-drift and not get dug out until spring. The McCunes probably had a huge freezer full of food that would last until June.

And there were always the brownies. The nose-tickling smell of baking brownies drifted into the hall.

"Do I smell brownies?" asked Jilly, sniffing, coming downstairs. She was followed by the twins dressed in matching pink warm-up outfits, pink bows in their powdery-gray brown curls. "That's the best smell in the whole world." She took a deep breath and licked her lips.

Peanut didn't have a chance to answer. There was a thumping and a banging on the front porch and a scrape-scrape-scrape.

Bong! The doorbell sounded.

She put her face against the glass and peered out into the winter darkness. The snowdrift blocking the door was gone. Someone was out there, someone in a parka. She couldn't tell who it was. "Do you suppose it's okay to open the door?" she asked. Opening the door to strangers was one of the things you never did when you baby-sat.

"Put on the chain," suggested Jilly. "Nobody can get past that."

69

Peanut hooked the chain and opened the door a crack.

"Hi, Goober," said a familiar voice from inside the parka. "Is my sister in there?"

"It's Jerry," said Peanut, fooling with the chain to get the door open.

"Jerry! What's he doing here?" asked Jilly. What could her brother possibly want? Why had he come? To tease them? Jerry teased more than any brother any girl anywhere ever had to put up with.

Peanut got the chain unlatched and pulled the door open.

A snow shovel leaned against the porch railing. Next to it was a pair of skis. Snow was piled high on each side of the path leading up to the porch. The steps were cleared off. So was the space around the front door.

Jerry stamped snow off his feet and came inside. "Haven't had a chance to use my skis since last winter." He pushed back his parka hood. "Hey, Jilly — I just came to see if you guys were okay."

Jilly stared. Jerry was worried about her?

He rubbed and slapped his hands to warm

them. "I mean, this is some blizzard. Dad and Mom might not get home from Rockford until late. I thought you could use a man around here."

Whatever for? She and Peanut were getting along just fine.

Suddenly it came to Jilly, an incredible idea: Jerry the Prune thought she might be in trouble. Jerry was being an un-prune. He was being nice, really nice! It was all so strange she hardly knew what to say.

Then she thought of the snow-cleared path, of the snowless steps and porch. "It sure is great, the way you shoveled the walk and everything," she said shyly.

"Aw, it was no big deal," said Jerry. "Not for someone with muscles."

"Thanks, Big Brother," said Jilly.

Jerry looked proud and not quite sure of what to say. Jilly had never called him Big Brother before.

Maggie came from the kitchen just then. "The brownies are cooling. We can eat them pretty soon."

"Want a brownie," said Bridget.

"Me, too," said Deirdre.

Peanut's mouth watered. There was nothing better than a fresh, still-warm brownie.

"You know," Jerry said thoughtfully, "the walk around the side of the house still needs to be shoveled. I guess I'll go do that."

"I'll come with you," said Maggie. "I just love being out in the snow." She ran to get her things from the back hall. Her voice carried into the front of the house. "Meet you outside."

Nibbsie could always tell when someone was getting ready to go outside. He skittered toward the kitchen, yipping.

"Maggie, will you take Nibbsie with you?" called Peanut. "I think he needs to go out."

"Okay," came Maggie's answer.

"Don't let him get lost in a deep snowbank," Peanut cautioned her.

Maggie didn't need to be told that. She didn't answer.

Jerry pulled his parka hood around his face and stepped out onto the porch.

Jilly leaned out into the cold. "Come back in for a brownie when you're finished, Jer."

"Just one?" came his answer. "Just a measly one?"

Now that was Jerry being a tease. Jilly didn't answer. She closed the door firmly.

The twins were hopping around Peanut. "Brownies?" they begged. "Brownies?"

"Oh, first we've got to have some real food," said Peanut. Hey — she was sounding exactly like her mother.

The corners of the twins' mouths turned down.

"I know something good," said Jilly. "I just love" — she put her face close to theirs, her eyes round, and spoke in a whisper — "hot dogs and beans."

The corners of the twins' mouths tipped upward.

"And I know where we can get some," said Peanut, heading toward the kitchen.

The telephone rang as she passed it. It was Mrs. Matthews. Peanut handed it to Jilly and went on her way, trying not to step on the twins, who had forgotten about brownies.

"Hot doggies," they chanted. "Yummmmm."

"My mom says they're at a motel in Elgin," said Jilly, coming into the kitchen. "The Interstate is closed. Nothing's getting through. They can't get home until tomorrow. Was she ever glad to hear Jerry is here. And she says can he sleep at your house tonight? I can, too," she added, as she got the twins' cover-ups and began putting them on.

"Let's us have hot dogs, too," said Peanut. "There's enough in the fridge for everybody."

"You know," said Jilly, "I don't think we should try to eat when the twins do. Let's feed them first." She eyed the pink warm-up suits. "It would be a shame to get those cute outfits all beany."

Peanut shuddered. "Another bath," she said. "More clothes changing."

"I wonder what Mrs. McCune will say when she sees all those clothes in the hamper," said Jilly, pouring milk.

"She'll know we took really good care of her twins," said Peanut.

"I wonder if she'll know that it was pretty hard," said Jilly. "Do you suppose they always get into so much mischief?"

"Toilet water!" said Peanut.

They exploded with laughter.

It wasn't easy, keeping the twins bean-free. They didn't want to be fed. They were big girls, they said. They ate all by themselves, they said. See? they said, picking up pieces of hot dog with their fingers and aiming for their mouths. Sometimes they made it on the first try.

Peanut groaned a lot. Then she solved the problem. She got stacks of wet towels so that she and Jilly could mop up fingers and faces after every bite.

The hands of the kitchen clock stood at five-thirty. The McCunes still hadn't come home.

Six o'clock came and went. Maggie and Jerry came inside. Peanut and Jilly set the table, and the four of them ate while the twins played near the kitchen window, where Peanut could keep an eye on them.

"This is good," said Jerry. "Man, I'm hungry."

"Shoveling snow is hard work," said Maggie.

"Pizza would have been better," Peanut said wistfully.

"I'll bet nobody's eating pizza tonight," said Jerry. "Nothing was moving on the streets when I came. Cars are stuck everywhere. Delivery trucks wouldn't stand a chance of getting through."

"Do you suppose the McCunes are stuck somewhere?" asked Jilly.

The twins' heads lifted. They lost interest in their dolls. Their faces puckered.

"Mommy?"

"I want my mommy."

Peanut hoisted Bridget — safety-pinned Bridget — onto her shoulder and headed for the living room, singing softly. "Hush, little baby, don't you cry. Peanut's going to sing you a lullaby."

Jilly followed, cuddling Deirdre. "And when that lullaby is through, Peanut's going to . . . going to . . . " She looked desperately at Peanut.

"Peanut's going to pick you up and say boo!"

The twins giggled.

The song went on, stanza after stanza, as Peanut and Jilly settled down on the sofa.

76

". . . a cow to say moo." ". . . an owl to call whooo." ". . . the dove that says coo."

The little girls grew quiet. The song went on forever, with the rhymes becoming more and more weird. ". . . take you to the zoo." ". . . show you a bird that flew." ". . . tell you what we'll do." ". . . oh, phoooo, because I can't think of any more rhymes."

It didn't matter. The twins' eyes had closed.

Eight o'clock passed. Peanut and Jilly sat on the sofa beside the sleeping twins, watching television. Maggie and Jerry sat on the window seat, looking out at the snow, talking, talking, talking in low voices.

"What do you think they're talking about?" whispered Peanut.

"*Why* do you suppose they're talking?" Jilly whispered back. "I mean — why?"

"Maybe they like each other."

Oh, that couldn't be. Maggie like Jerry? Jerry like Maggie? Girls and boys who liked each other were glamorous, like people in a story. Maggie and Jerry weren't glamorous the way Fred and Ginger were. They were just Peanut and Jilly's sister and brother. They

78

were probably talking because there was nothing else to do. . . .

A long time after the clock on the mantel dinged out nine times, Peanut began to wonder if they were going to get to stay up and watch the late-late show. She had always wanted to watch the late-late show. Maybe it was full of grown-up things. Wasn't it time she got to know about such things?

Suddenly there was a sound at the front door. She ran to open it. Mrs. Roman stepped inside, bringing a blast of cold air with her. "My dear," she said, "you will never know what I've gone through. I was brought here by a police car! The officers were so kind when they heard what I was upset about. They brought me right to the corner of Main Street and — "

Peanut didn't hear the rest. There was another thumping on the porch. It was Mrs. Butterman. "I thought I'd never get here!" she said, dropping her coat on the hall bench and rubbing her hands. "Believe it or not, the train was stuck. A snowplow engine finally came and cleared the tracks in front of us all the way to Evanston. I walked from the station. Cars aren't moving. Only people are."

She looked around. "Has everything been all right here?"

All right. Did that mean not having a makeup mess or a bath powder blitz? Or did it mean taking care of everything when the problems happened? Peanut answered in the only way she could. "I was in charge, Mom. Why wouldn't everything be all right?"·

Mrs. Butterman gave her a quick squeeze and glanced into the living room. "Maggie! You're here! How nice. But don't tell me the McCunes aren't home yet!"

"And I only just got here," said Mrs. Roman. "This has to be the blizzard of the decade."

Even as she spoke a key turned in the lock and the front door opened.

"Home at last," sighed Mrs. McCune. "We got stuck on the Outer Drive. And then we got stuck on Sheridan Road. How many times, dear?" she asked, turning to Mr. McCune.

He shrugged out of his coat. "Lost count. We're lucky we got as far as we did before we had to give up on the car." He looked around at everybody. "We," he said, "hoofed it all the way from South Boulevard."

"Is everything all right?" asked Mrs. Mc-Cune.

There it was again, that question. It must be terrible to be a grown-up and think that wherever you weren't, ghastly things were happening! Peanut didn't even try to answer. "The twins are asleep on the sofa," she said instead.

Mrs. McCune went to look. "There they are," she crooned, kissing them. "They didn't give you any trouble, did they?"

Trouble? Trouble! Why spoil Mrs. McCune's homecoming? "Nothing I couldn't take care of," said Peanut.

"Aren't they darling in pink?" said Mrs. Butterman. "You ought to dress them in that color all the time."

"They look like little angels," murmured Mrs. Roman.

One of the "angels" opened her eyes. She had the dreamy look of someone who isn't really awake. "You rat," she sighed. "You dirty rat." Her eyes fluttered shut.

Peanut gulped.

"Pickle juice!" Jilly breathed softly.

Mrs. McCune blinked. "Now where in the world can she have heard that? I'm going to have to keep them away from the television set, that I can see."

CHAPTER
8

"Mom?" They were on their way home. The snow had stopped. The wind had died. The night world glistened with whiteness. "Did you ever go to Parents' School?" asked Peanut. She had wondered about that all day.

"Parents' School?" Her mother didn't understand.

"You know," said Peanut, "where you learned to say things like 'No cookies till you finish your peas,' and 'Don't slam the door,' and 'Can you say thank you?' "

Mrs. Butterman shook her head. "I learned from my mother. Even though you don't know it, you're learning from me."

Nibbsie wiggled to get down. Peanut held him tight. "No, Nibbs," she said, "I'm not putting you down no matter how much you wiggle. The snow is too deep for you to run in."

"What I just heard," said Mrs. Butterman, "is you sounding like Nibbsie's mother."

Well! Peanut had never thought about that.

"You do what's best for whomever you're responsible for."

Peanut had done her best for Bridget and Deirdre.

Tomorrow she was going to have to tell Mrs. McCune about the bath powder and all those clothes in the hamper and the makeup. Oh! She had forgotten about the streaky mirror above the dressing table. And the "toilet" water. Was Mrs. McCune ever going to be surprised when she saw the mirror and looked for her cologne!

Peanut and Jilly were walking with Mrs.

Butterman, lifting their feet high out of the snow with each step. Maggie and Jerry were ahead of them, sliding along smoothly on their skis.

"Know something, Mom?" Peanut said softly. "Maggie and Jerry like each other."

"How nice," said Mrs. Butterman.

"But it's so funny," said Jilly.

"Why *funny?*"

"Well, it's not a bit like a story — you know, falling in love and all that. It's just Maggie."

"And Jerry," added Jilly.

"But that's how it happens," said Mrs. Butterman. "You mustn't tease them."

The snow lay over everything like a soft, silk coverlet.

"I've got to make a snow angel," said Peanut. "Just one. Please — will you hold Nibbsie?"

Mrs. Butterman took him and Peanut made a perfect snow angel.

Jilly made another beside it.

"I've never done that at night," said Peanut. "I wonder if it'll still be here tomorrow."

"It's magic outside," Jilly said softly. "I'm

going to paint a picture of snow at night."

Peanut took Nibbsie back. She thought of something else. "I wonder if I'll ever like a boy. Like that, I mean."

"I don't think I will," said Jilly.

"I like Nate and David and even old Ollie," said Peanut. "But they're . . . like . . . you know . . . my friends, my buddies."

"Someday," Mrs. Butterman said softly, "someday you each will meet a boy you'll think is extra special. You'll want to share good times with him. The good times will be even better because he's there."

How would all that feel? Peanut couldn't imagine.

"And what's more," said Mrs. Butterman as they turned into the yard, "those boys are going to feel that exact same way about you."

Really? Peanut and Jilly thought their own separate thoughts as they went up the steps. This was something they were going to have to talk about later, when they were in bed.

Mrs. Butterman unlocked the door and they all went inside.

Outside, on the porch, two pairs of skis leaned against the wall.

The clouds parted. The moon came out. And the snow glittered all around the house.

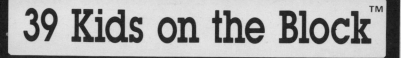